David Wingate

Poems and Songs by David Wingate

David Wingate

Poems and Songs by David Wingate

ISBN/EAN: 9783744711982

Printed in Europe, USA, Canada, Australia, Japan

Cover: Foto ©Andreas Hilbeck / pixelio.de

More available books at **www.hansebooks.com**

POEMS AND SONGS

BY

DAVID WINGATE,

AUTHOR OF LILY NEIL, ANNIE WEIR, &c., &c.

GLASGOW:
KERR & RICHARDSON,
1883.

PREFACE.

I TRUST the reader knows that I have several times hoped the Public—those of it who read books—would think I did well in publishing certain volumes of Verses, and I shall be sorry if it is thought by a large number that I am doing wrong now. But any regrets of that kind which I may have by and by cannot be written here. To my Subscribers I owe thanks, and here express them very sincerely; and to all those who defer purchasing till they see what sort of a bargain they are to have, I say, God grant that it please them.

Respectfully,

DAVID WINGATE.

GOVANHILL, GLASGOW,
February, 1883.

CONTENTS.

Out among the Oaks of Cadzow.

THE BALLAD-MAKERS.

YONDER is the noble river,
　　Shimmering through the forest thin;
Listen to its song of welcome,
　　Murmur'd with a laugh-like din:
Bright as April, when the summer
　　Comes before sweet May has come,
When the sloes with bloom are snowy,
　　And the bees about them hum.

Here in Avon's gleam reclining
　　In the beeches' shadow wide,
While the warder-firs salute us,
　　Bowing from the further side;

While the tassell'd larches, whispering,
    Of a stranger's presence tell,
And the startled roebuck, bounding,
    Bears the tidings down the dell.

After flasks and pipes refresh us,
    Who's our chosen bard to-day?
His the choice of song or story,
    Ours to bear it as we may;
But with Avon's self to listen,
    And its birds the leaves among,
Surely ne'er were fitter audience;
    Is it ballad, bard, or song?

THE BALLAD.

ONCE upon a time a lady,
    Fair as life when Love's new born,
Left her proud impatient palfrey
    Bound to yonder hoary thorn:
Not the forest flowers to gather,
    Not the forest merles to hear,
Nor the tale of favour'd wooer,
    Murmur'd in a willing ear.

See among the bushes yonder,
  By the weedy wagon-way,
Low among the broken brackens,
  Sits a woman old and grey.
Desolate she seems and crazy,
  Thin as death and rheumy-eyed,
And the fair and noble lady
  Whispers, bending at her side:

" Mother—let me call you mother,
  Since you are so old and frail—
Wherefore are you here so often,
  Sitting lonely thus and pale?
I am in the forest riding
  Morn and e'en and every day,
And I never fail to meet you,
  Mourning, somewhere on my way.

" Even at home your presence haunts me,
  In my slumbers you are there;
In the evening dance you mingle,
  Mourning, mourning everywhere.

" Oh, if you would only trust me,
    I, a prying girl that seem,
May be more an angel coming
    Unaware than you can deem.

" Haply in the river's babble,
    Mother, you some solace find;
For the voice of running water
    Soothes, they say, a weary mind.
But it is a wayward river,
    Changing oft from smiles to wrath;
And to dare its strength resembles
    Sitting in the lightning's path.

'. You have heard its reckless rushing,
    When its sources send it down
Like a sea-wave, tempest driven,
    Thunder torrents thick and brown;
While its boulders roll'd before it,
    And its hazels dripp'd with spray;
Long the thunder has been booming,
    Mother, up the strath to-day.

" Nay, if 'tis a secret sorrow,
    Still from me let it be so,
  Sacred in your bosom keep it;
    Wherefore should a stranger know?
But the setting sunbeams faintly
    Gilds the trees on yonder hill, ·
And the river-mist is rising,
    And the air is growing chill;

" Therefore, let me urge you, mother,
    Though unkind it seems and rude
Thus to teaze you with my presence,
    Let me help you from the wood.
Cold and cramp will else assail you,
    For at night they linger here;
And the burden of your sorrow
    Surely is enough to bear."

" Gin ye be sae aften ridin' "
    (Thus the mourner) " down the glen,
Maybe, leddy, ye can tell me,
    A' that lang I've socht to ken;

" Hae ye ever seen my Athur?—
   He was rosy as yoursel'.
Hae ye ever seen him, leddy,
   Doon aboot in glade or dell?

" Athur's lost, the neebors tell me—
   Lost an' gane this mony a day;
An' they think his mither's crazy,
   When she trows nae what they say.
Think ye God wad let a mither
   Sae her only callan tyne?
Nae! the thocht but wrangs oor Maker—
   Yet he's ne'er been hame sinsyne.

" Ne'er sinsyne I've seen him, leddy;
   Oh, a cruel thing it seems!
But he wadnae aye be comin'
   Lauchin' to me in my dreams—
Heaven would ne'er wi' leein' visions
   Mock a mournin' heart like mine,
Gin my laddie werenae leevin'—
   But he's ne'er been hame sinsyne.

" Dootless ye hae heard the story?
 Wha but's heard it? Wha but's been
Peerin' in the darkness yonder
 Whare there's naething to be seen?
There, they say, his ghaist is hauntin',
 Benward aye it seems to glide;
But the ghaist is nane o' Willie's,
 Else frae me it wadnae hide.

" Gin I could but trow my laddie
 'Neath the braes is lyin' yet,
Then I michtnae doot his speerit
 In aboot the mines micht flit.
Maybe watchin' owre his body
 Till a prayer aboon't be sain,
Or, at least, a kin'ly finger
 On his sichtless een be lain.

" Mony a weary year sin', leddy,
 While the shearers swat and sang,
Word cam' to the field that something
 Doon aboot the pit was wrang— .

" 'Athur Aedie wannert someway,'
    That was a' they seem'd to ken;
' Athur Aedie wannert someway,'
    Has been whisper'd aye since then.

" Dootless ye hae heard the story,
    Hoo for weeks an' weeks they socht,
Days an' sleepless nichts, unwearit—
    But their toilin' naething brocht.
Aye for langer search cam' reasons,
    Better reasons aye again,
But o' wannert Athur Aedie
    Trace or tidings gat they nane.

" Then the searchers sicken'd, weary,
    An' they took the bluid hounds in,
As if they wi' Doom were playin',
    An' the game had sworn to win.
Muckle frae the hounds they houpit—
    Mair than they could houp to hae;
Could the feet o' Athur Aedie,
    Guide a filthy beast o' prey?

"Then the river pools they raiket,
  A' the shallows waded syne,
Then they dared unheard o' dangers,
  Turnin' fa's within the mine.
Clyde they socht, and Cadzow's ruins,
  Doon the cradled well an' a',
But I never thocht it likely
  Athur in the well would fa'.

"Through the oaks, their clefts and hollows
  Searchin', days an' nichts they ran;
E'en the wildest thocht was welcome—
  Wisdom seem'd in every plan.
Aye the search grew wide an' wider—
  Weariness ne'er cost a care;
But the mair they search'd the louder
  Croak'd the raven o' Despair.

"But they never saw him, leddy,
  Athur Aedie wasna there;
Heaven—ye maunna think I haver—
  Heaven had Athur in its care.

" An' although it keeps him hidden,
　　Aft it seems a sin to fret,
When sae mony blithesome visions
　　Tell me aye he's leevin' yet.

" Dootless ye hae heard about it,
　　They've been tellin't far an' near:
Ah! but I hae things to tell o',
　　That abroad ye canna hear;
Whiles its like an auld-warld story,
　　That I only trow has been;
Whiles it seems my rosy callan
　　Only gaed awa' yestreen.

" Mony a nicht his faither's wi' me,
　　And sae life-like does he seem,
That I kenna if I'm dreamin',
　　Or but waukent frae a dream.
Owre again we hear oor callan,
　　By the eastlin' winnock gaun,
Or the sneck we hear him liftin',
　　Aye whene'er we lay us doon.

" Owre again his faither seeks him,
 Roun' an' roun' the toun at e'en,
Thinkin' he was maybe hidin',
 Feart yet willin' to be seen.
Owre again he seems, when wildly
 Roars the win' an' pours the rain,
Careless o' himsel' to seek him,
 Oot an' in an' oot again.

" Owre again at nicht we linger,
 Till the lamp is glimmerin' dim,
Waitin' for the foot that never
 Enters bringin' news o' him.
Or the fire we hear him chappin',
 Noo, as then, we thocht we heard;
Or about the loan we hear him
 Liltin' like a mornin' bird.

" Oh! gin I were only dreamin'!
 Thin his faither grew an' wan,
Then to speak o' meetin' Athur
 'Mang the angels he began;

"Then he laid him doon an' waited
  Patient till the word was sain;
Then the neebours in the mornin'
  Cam', and my gudeman was gane.

"Oh! but its an unco' story,
  An' there's muckle mair to tell,
Dreams o' sorrow born, owre awfu'
  E'en to think o' by mysel'.
Grief, they say, the tongue will lowsen,
  An' it may be true in pairt,
But the deepest sorrow silent
  Sits an' gnaws awa' the heart.

"Leddy, let us kneel thegither,
  Oh, but ye are unco kin',
Pray for tidin's o' my Athur,
  An' my thochts wi' yours will join:
Say his mither's heart is breakin',
  Say that Death 's been near her gaun
Mony a day, an' aye in pity
  Hauds his aften-lifted haun'.

"Tell *Him* o' her unco yearnin'
　　Day an' nicht an' morn an' e'en;
Why He lets the King o' Terrors
　　Spare her say ye canna ween.
Speir if it be but to bless her
　　Wi' her bairn's return again;
Spier if it be but to show her
　　Houp was never born in vain.

"Beg o' Him a sign, kin' leddy,—
　　Signs we maybe shouldna seek,
But the King o' Heaven nae langer
　　Deigns wi' folk on earth to speak.
Beg ye then a sign, sweet leddy,
　　Sic as Heaven alane can gie;
Wherefore should He keep me waitin'
　　When a sign would set me free?

"Thrice let Athur pass before us,
　　An' if he be dead an' gane,
Let him be a callan smilin'
　　In his mither's face fu' fain.

" Thrice, if he be leevin', let him
　　Pass a broon an' bearded man,
　Ploddin' hame to tell his faither
　　Hoo, an' why, and whare he ran.

" Wait awee wi' patience, leddy,
　　Fauld your haun's an' wait awee;
　Bearded man or smilin' callan
　　Dootless we, belyve, will see;
` Gin there be an ear aboon us,
　　That can hear us when we pray,
　Gin there be a God to answer,
　　Leddy, we'll an answer hae.

" Oh! but I am unco dizzy—
　　Aften I am dizzy noo,
　Aften I hae stoons like burnin'
　　Arrows dartin' through my broo;
　Aften I am blin' a weeock,
　　An' a glimmerin' fills my een,
　Like the skinkle o' the moonbeams
　　On the frozen snaw that's seen.

" Neither man nor callan passes!
 Leddy, ye hae pray'd in vain;
What ava's the guid o' prayin'
 If to answer there be nane?
Nocht's for me but weary waitin';
 Ah! but frettin's wrang in me—
Maybe I am keepit waitin'
 Just to kiss him or I dee.

" Fare-ye-weel! forget me, leddy; .
 . Whyles my words are wrang I fear;
Leddies shouldna hear o' troubles
 That may gar them drap a tear.
Dinna ye wi' thinkin' o' me
 Darken ither glens an streams;
Drive me frae your thochts an', maybe,
 God will keep me frae your dreams."

Then, a path among the bushes
 Choosing, up the braes she wound,
Ever searchin', ever searchin',
 Searchin' with a faith profound;

Never fancy's fond assurance
· Yieldin' wholly to despair,
But a melancholy pleasure
Findin' in her constant care.

At the Milken well she linger'd,
Listening to its murmur low,
Listening to the tale it told her
Of the summers long ago:
Of the happy, sunny summers,
Yet so like a pleasant dream,
When her rosy callan, daily,
Came to its unfailing stream.

Thus they parted; but the purling
Of the Milken well shall cease,
And no more for ever, Avon,
Sing its summer song of peace;
And the stillness of the olden
Times to Quarter come again,
Ere the fate of Athur Aedie
Cease a wonder to remain.

"Wha but has some Athur Aedie?"
  Thus we said when closed the tale;
"Wha but has some Athur Aedie
  O' the fancy to bewail?—
Something ever bright and distant
  Lov'd and vainly long'd for still,
Like a gem unpriced that sparkles
  On a high and pathless hill."

Puir Wee Davie: A Winter Lay.

DEDICATED TO THE SCHOOL BOARDS.

PUIR wee Davie,
  He's up before the sun,
    An' oot an' paidlin' through the snaw,
      Or battlin' wi' the win';
For Davie's aucht year auld an' mair,
  An' sae, come o't what will,
Be't cauld or warm, through calm and storm,
  He maun be at the schule.

An' Davie aye frae morn to e'en
    Is wi' his lessons thrang,
An' though he's never praised when richt,
    He's blamed eneuch when wrang.
They gar him try a hunner things,
    An' if he fails in ane,
They're at him wi' the tawse, or waur,
    Till dark he's "*keepit in.*"

Puir wee Davie,
    He maun be oot gin nine,
An' till the sun's ahint the hill
    He ne'er wins back to dine.
An' aft when creepin' hame he hears
    The man that's in the moon
Say saftly to his neebor starns,
    "That bairn's been "*keepit in.*"

An' though nae waur than ither bairns,
    His fauts come aye aboon;
He's leuking wrang, or sitting wrang,
    Or makin' needless din;

Or maybe while the maister prays,
   Wi' ae hauf-open ee,
Wee Davie's seen to smile—then doon
   For " *keepin' in*" is he.

Puir wee Davie,
   His heart is aften fou,
An', tearfu', he his troubles tells
   Wi' tremblin' voice an' mou'.
He thinks the maister's spitefu'—
   Just the warst that e'er he saw—
An' wonners what he means to mak'
   By " *keepin' in*" ava'.

But though till nicht he's " *keepit in*,"
   He's no yet free frae schule,
His taties ta'en—he's thrang again
   On table, chair, or stool:
There's coonts to dae—hame coonts, they say,—
   An' adjectives to fin',
An' screeds frae printit books to write—
   His wark is never done.

Puir wee Davie,
   Fu' brawly he can spell,
An' read—what is't he canna read?—
   An' nouns frae verbs can tell.
An' though sic things in aulder brains
   Micht weel confusin' be,
Yet Davie's nouns and Davie's verbs
   Maun never disagree.

Puir wee Davie,
   It's pityfu' to see
The wolf o' sorrow worryin'
   A bairn sae wan an' wee,
An' hear him speak o' "weary warlds,"
   Like ane that's struggled lang,
An' sees frae trouble nae relief—
   There maun be something wrang.

Although his big blue ee's sae bright,
   He's nocht but skin and bane,
He croichles when he's cauld, and aft
   Has in his side a pain.

An' though he's rosy when he rins,
  Or goufs about his ba',
His bits o' cheeks are lily-pale
  As soon's the fun's awa'.

Oh ye! our honour'd " Board," weel-waled,
  Wha tax us as ye will,
Why mak' ye, in your zeal for lair,
  A hothouse o' the schule,
.Whare bairns, like plants in raws arranged,
  Maun ere their season blaw,
To swell the maister-gar'ner's fame
  An' win a prize or twa.

An' ye (if sic there be), whase care
  (It's best to write it plain)
Is ne'er a scholar's health, but hoo
  A croon o' "*grant*" to gain,
Hae mercy! Dinna grudge a lauch,
  If usefu' wark be done,
An' *min'* ye may owre-task a bairn
  An' kill wi' "*keepin' in.*"

But, patience! Puir wee Davie!
 They needna owre ye craw!
Your mither kens about a plan
 Will pay them back for't a':
When roon the stern Inspector comes
 To see what way ye've done,
She'll jist sen' owre a line, an' say
 " *Wee Davie's keepit in.*"

In the Glen of Dalziel.

"OH! ken ye wha has left us?"
 Said the Woodruff to the Fern,
 "Oh! ken ye wha has left us?
  E'en the laird's sweet laddie-bairn.
Never mair amang the starworts
 In the sunshine he'll be seen,
Wi' his hauns as white's my petals,
 And his bonny glancin' e'en;
For they've laid him in the shadow
 That nae sunbeam lichts, I ween.

"Hae ye heard the waefu' wailin'
   O' the linties, Lady Fern?
Hae ye heard their waefu' wailin'
   For the laird's lost laddie-bairn?
E'en the kaes are chatterin' saftly,
   An' the robin sings, they say,
As he sings in dull October,
   When the grass is turnin' grey—
As when ne'er a flower can hear him
   On a cheerless winter day.

"Heard ye ocht like some ane sabbin',
   Lady Fern, fu' late yestreen,
When the stars we saw were glimmerin'
   In the lift like tearfu' een?
While the ivy leaves were flappin'
   A' alang the kirk-yaird wa',
An' the dew, like tears, aboot us
   Frae the trees began to fa'—
Heard ye ocht like some ane sabbin',
   Lady Fern, yestreen ava?

" "Twas his mither's sel' was passin',
   Wae and weary up the glen,
In sic grief as only mithers
   Wha hae lost like her can ken.
There are kindly hearts aboot her
   That to see her tears are sair;
An' there's ae dear ane that blythely
   On himsel' would tak' her care;
But the cup o' grief's nae sweeter
   Though a mournin' world may share.

"Oh! gin we micht but tell her,
   While she's wailin', Lady Fern,
That the flowers she'll see neist summer
   But precede her bonny bairn;
We micht wile her frae her sorrow,
   And wi' this micht dry her ee—
He but lies a langer winter
   In the lichtless gloom than we;
But the summer will be endless
   When your bairn you neist shall see."

The Minister's Corn.

THE minister's corn was a crap as good
  As ere on the riggs o' the glebe had stood,
  And the sparrows that aye 'mang the ears
    were seen
Were sacred birds in the minister's een—
For the grubs they kept doon in the spring," quoth he,
And there's plenty for them and there's plenty for me."

Oh! bright was the day when the minister's man,
And the minister's lassie the hairst began,
Wi' the helpin' o' neebors twa or three;
But the weather was fickle as fickle could be;
An' though there were rainbows at nicht and at morn,
Yet dreich was the hairst o' the minister's corn.

But the blast that was laden wi' rain blew oot,
And a drouthy win' cam' frae the wast aboot,
And soof't a blythe sang in the leafy nooks,
And linger'd to drink by the drookit stooks,
Till the sheaves were as dry as dry could be,
And rustled an' shook in the win' wi' glee.

But the minister's corn was hurried in,
On a threatening morning, a day owre soon—
A day owre soon, for the cloud blew by,
And the drouthy win' ruled for a week in the sky.

Then oot in the morning—aye early was he—
The minister wandered, and what did he see?
But a wavering cloud whare nae cloud should be;
Nae cloud but itsel' in the breeze was borne,
And whare was its source?—e'en his ain *stack o' co*

Oh! weel micht the minister sigh, I wat,
For nae *sillar* linin' hae clouds like that.
But, "Swith! ca' the lassie! and, Swith! ca' the m
Gae get a' the neebors aboot that ye can!
For if it be drouthy or if it be rain,
The stack maun be doon and in stooks again!"
Man, neebor, and lassie to help ran fain,
For the minister aye had a mind o' his ain.
And sae when the win' drank the dew o' the morn
Ance mair in the stook was the minister's corn.

Aye, muckle gude grain has been scatter'd," quoth he,
But we hae't a' amang us—the sparrows and me."
ut the sun shone oot and the win' blew fair
ill the minister's corn was in stack ance mair.

erene in his study the minister leaned,
'here the ever-ripe hairst o' his thoughts he gleaned:
was a Saturday e'en—wearin' near the Lord's Day—
nd the minister's fancy had soared away
o that far happy land where the matter's all mind,
nd the grossest of creatures a being refined.
long the host o' the happy some few that had been
  his flock on the earth he discovered, I ween;
r his bright eye grew brighter, and "Wha's yon I.
    see?
ave toiled not in vain for the MASTER," quoth he.
ome grains I hae garner'd, if some hae been lost,
e proof o't is yonder in yon happy host."
t back to the earth (they wha can may explain
hy a thought flies so fast) flashed his fancy again,
t back to his flock, yet on this side the "*bourne*,"
t back to the glebe, and his ain stack o' corn."

Then, " Oh for a thrasher," he sighed, " wha could lay
The grain o' the glebe in a heap in one day;
But there's no such a thrasher"—when opens the door,
And the weeest o' mannikins steps up the floor;
Three spans was his stature, his beard half as lang,
And his tongue when he spoke had an east country
    twang;
His claes were o' moleskin wi' buttons o' pearl,
But his bearin' micht weel hae been owned by an earl
He took aff his bonnet, and lootin' awee,
" Gudeman, was ye wantin' a thrasher?" quoth he.

The minister rose when he first saw the sicht,
And thinkin' he hardly was seein' aricht,
" What are ye? What want ye? Whence come ye?
    he cried.
" Was ye wantin' a thrasher?" the dwarfie replied.
The minister stared; quoth the dwarfie again,
" Gin a thrasher ye're wantin', I ken whare there's ane

The minister smiled—for a mortal it seemed
(Though sae wee), and its ee like a human ee gleamed

(Though a wee blinkie brichter than maist human een).
Quoth the minister, "Aye! that do I, my wee frien',
But a thousand like you I hae wark for, I ween."

'.But, hooly gudeman, I'm nae thrasher mysel',
But whare ye'll get ane 'tis my errand to tell;
And them that I serve sent me yont jist to say,
Ye've ane that will thrash a' your grain in a day."

   "And what for a day
    O' your man maun I pay?
ome bargain unholy I fear it may be;
   Maun the price be a soul?
   Ane?—or maybe the whole
f the souls in the parish are wanted," quoth he.

he mannikin leuch—"Oh, gudeman, ye're astray,
'e've nae traffic in souls, sir."
            "Then what maun I pay?"
A bucket o' water as saft as may be,
r an aizle, puir chiel, in his thrapple has he;
nd a bushel o' coal a' as clean as ye can,
r the thrasher is dainty o' 's eatin', gudeman;

But spare nae the water and scrimp nae the coal,
For hunger and drouth's what oor man canna thole.
Shall we send ye oor thrasher?"

                 "You may."

                        "Then the morn
Be ready wi' horses to ca' in your corn."
"The morn!" cried the minister.

                        "Tyesday then say,"
Quoth the dwarf, "and hae plenty o' hauns for the
    strae."
And then wi' a loot slow and laigh he was gane,
And the minister lean'd in his study alane.

The dawn o' the Tyesday was hardly awa
Till the thrasher appeared in his carriage an twa,
And servants that bustled and waled him a place
Whare the stoor o' the strae wadnae blaw in his face;
Whare the spire o' the kirk through the elms micht be
    seen,
And a glint o' the manse through the holly sae green.
And they gied him a taste o' the water sae clear,
And they fed him wi' coal frae a heugh that was near.

But the minister's helpers wi' wonder grew pale,
While the thrasher was bound wi' strong whangs to
    his flail.
"For hoo can he work in sic bonds?" was their plea.
"Hoo work?" said his servants, "Hae patience and
    see;
And noo he's at wark—Fie! mair hauns let us hae!
'Twill take a gude dozen to redd him o' strae;
Gae! get us mair pocks ere the grain rin to waste,"
And the minister's sel' for mair pocks gaed in haste.

And weel micht the minister marvel, I ween,
For never before had sic thrashing been seen;
And weel micht he say, "Is it glamour or no?"
But these were his helpers that ran to an' fro;
And there was the lassie, and yonder the man,
She rosy wi' toil, and he pechin' an' wan',
And there swell'd the grain heaps, and there rose the
   strae.
The thrasher, unwearied, there rattled away,
And he seem'd to grow stronger the more work was
    done;
The breath of his nostrils oft darkening the sun,

And, o'er the Turnlaw while the sun yet was high,
The minister saw that the thrashin' was bye.

At rest stood the thrasher: his bonds were unbound;
And the still wondering helpers were gather'd around;
The coal was removed that remain'd in his maw—
It was hot as a furnace the pale helpers saw;
But the fumes of the brunstone hot stifling arose,
Till the helpers were fain to run holding the nose.
And, lo! from the thrasher an ear-cracking roar
Made the hazel leaves quiver the valley all o'er;
And, see, on the Dechmont the kine, startled, run,
As the breath o' the thrasher shuts out sky and sun.

Deep awe seized the helpers—their thoughts one
    might tell—
Ane said 'tis the fumes o' the *ill place* itsel';
And ane said the corn wad tak' fire in the kiln,
And the barley wad bleeze in the pat and the still.
        " And the fire-fate sae fell
          O' Gommorah itsel'
Micht fa' on the parish."   But ae canny dame
Declared 'twas the minister's sel' was to blame;

" And if brunstone and fire's to be scattered ava,"
Quoth she, " on the minister's sel' it maun fa',
For (wi' rev'rence be't spoken) he's sinned for us a'."
But the minister's man or the minister's maid
Brang word to the manse o' what a' body said,
And the minister smiled, " Silly bodies," quoth he,
" For the thresher's nae mair o' a demon than me."

But the miller himsel', when the corn was sent in,
" We'll try a bit bag o't," quoth he, " to begin ;"
But the sample was canny as canny could be ;
" I think we may venture the rest o't," quoth he.

Sae the meal was brang hame and the minister's man
To ca' on the helpers wi' preein's began ;
And the minister said, " Let them prov't in the pat,
For the proof o' the puddin's the preein', I wat ;"
And a' body tastit and a' body saw
That the thrasher was naething uncanny ava.
And ever sinsyne when the glebe is in grain,
The minister sends for the *thrasher* again.

C

The Holy Troke.

By BETTY GOSSIP.

OR Session owed a debt that cost
　　Owre twenty pounds a year,
　　And ay they moaned and fumed and groaned
　　As it grew waur to bear.
But at length there cam' a crisis
　　In oor kirk's affairs; for Fate
Decree'd a fearfu' less'nin'
　　O' the "offerings" at the "plate."

And the Pastor sent for Mr. Pence,
　　The man that kept the bag
(Atweel, 'twas but a bag in name,
　　A toom and useless rag).
"Dear Mr. Pence," quoth he, aff loof,
　　"This thing's between us twa;
But thirty-five a quarter, sir,
　　It winna do ava."

" It's rather mair," said Mr. Pence;
    The Pastor raised his haun—
" Hae patience, sir, for we maun hear
    Before we un'erstaun':—
The lassie's fee's to pay you see;
    When that is ta'en awa'
It's thirty-five a quarter,
    And it winna do ava.

" I cam' to ye a happy man,
    I married and sat doon;
My wife was ane ye a' approved—
    As guid's was in the toon—
As guid, but just as puir's mysel—
    Weel, noo, we're nine in a';
And on thirty-five a quarter—
    Sir, it winna do ava.

" I'm deep in debt—I'm awn yoursel'—
    My credit's on the swing;
Indeed, I fear my leaving here
    Is maist a settled thing—

Unless an effort can be made.
   That twenty odd you pay
As interest?   Utter nonsense!   Get
   The debt swept off, I say."

Puir Mr. Pence held up his hauns,
   Sprang up and syne sat doon,
"Your debt to me can wait," quoth he,
   "Till better times come roon;
But sweep five hunder pounds awa!
   Ye speak like ane possess't;
Oor off'rin's fa' awa like snaw!
   But, sir, I'll do my best."

"Now, that is wise," the Pastor said.
   "Just listen, Mr. Pence,
This plan of mine.   I'll make it thine,
   Thou King of Commonsense.
Get up a Holy Troke.   Invite
   Free friends frae near and far."
"'Tuts, sir, ye joke!   What's 'Holy Troke?'"
   "Oh, it's a Church Bazaar.

"Get up a Holy Troke, I say,
  Take time and do it well,
Invite the fair ones of our Church
  To make, and beg, and sell;
And have a lady committee—
  My Jane will do her share—
And catch our worthy Provost's wife
  And put her in the chair.

"The lady element will toil
  Like oxen in the yoke.
But mind 'twill mar a Church Bazaar
  To ca't a 'Holy Troke.'
What say ye?" "Weel, I think the plan
  Will prove a perfit pet,
We'll trade in ocht, and pay for nocht,
  And haud by a' we get."

"Just so," the smiling Pastor said,
  "And when the debt is gane
And twenty pounds a-year set free
  I'll hae ye owre your lane,

For you're the man that hauds the bag,
　　Our chief man, Mr. Pence;
And five-and-twenty mair a-year
　　Ye ken's guid commonsense."

So Mr. Pence on some pretence
　　The session gat thegither,
And 'twas a lang and douce confab
　　They had wi' ane anither:
And syne they set their moles to work—
　　A' wormin' to a plan—
Some saw the Provost's wife, and some
　　Consulted her gudeman.

The Provost's wife—*hissel'*—for far
　　The better horse was she—
Got a' the ladies, young and auld,
　　To form a commit*tee.*
"Tak' ocht," she said, "but nice things first,
　　The brawest best will sell;
And to the lass that gathers maist
　　I'll gi'e a silver bell.

"Ye maunna beg for things.   Oh, no!—
　　My plan is better far—
　Hae e'en for a'; say ay, ' Hoo braw!
　　Hoo nice for oor Bazaar!'
And things that gentlemen would like
　　Ye'll wile frae gentlemen:
And them that really winna *give*,
　　They may be coax'd to len':

" For things that's lent, an' by mistake
　　Disposed o'—weel, ye see,
I dinna ken what can be said
　　If gentlemen they be—
We're workin' wi' a richteous aim,
　　As I am prood to tell:
But, yet, for a', wha maist can draw,
　　It's her will win the bell."

The day arrived.   A hall was hired,
　　(For, labourin' in the mirk,
Ae elder set his face against
　　Sic traffic in the kirk).

And there were tables round aboot
    Wi' glitterin' trifles braw,
And many a thocht in worsted wrocht
    Hung temptsome on the wa'.

And fifty smirkin' haun'-waled maids—
    At ilka table ane—
Were there to haun' the trifles oot,
    And haul the siller in.
And a'—the chairs, and tables e'en—
    Were priced on tickets neat;
It lacked but tickets on the maids
    To make the Troke complete.

Hoo weel the witchin' smile was plied,
    Hoo weel the pawky e'e,
Wi' lauchter licht frae morn to nicht—
    'Twas just a treat to see.
But what a dearth o' change there was
    Wad scarce be fair to tell,
For ilka maid had sworn, t'was said,
    That she wad win the bell.

At length the last geegaw's laid past,
  The hindmost scrap o' trash
Is sell't, and comes the happy hour
  When they may count the cash.
Some sware 'twas Bella Broon would win,
  And some said Maggie Hay,
For youths, moustached and crimson-sashed,
  Were near them a' the day.

At last the Provost's wife came in,
  Wi' gran' train trailin' roon,
Her dainty tablets in her haun',
  To note the drawin's doon;
And hoo they cheered her as she kissed
  Her winsome dochter Nell!
And, blushing, clasped upon her breast
  The tiny silver bell.

And syne a murmurin' souch gaed roon',
  Thus burdened—"Was it fair?
Wha kens what big a sum it cost
  To place the trophy there?"

And later on the ball-room shone
   (*The Assembly*, I should say),
Until the prying sun looked in
   On robes nae langer gay.

Then Mr. Pence, wha bann'd the ball
   Because he couldna dance,
Wi' twa-three mae, gaed owre to hae
   Some sherry at the manse;
And ere they left there was a purse
   Put in the pastor's haun',
Wi' guineas in't—a perfect mint,
   To him—ye un'erstaun?

And at the hindmost moment, just
   When troopin' frae the spence,
There was a graspin' o' the haun'
   O' pawky Mr. Pence;
And syne a whisperin' in his lug—
   "What think ye o' the joke?
Whare'er ye gang, if funds fa' wrang,
   Commend a Holy Troke."

By the Burn of Shield.

" COME tell us that tale of the brown-hair'd child,
  Who came to the stubble field,
And sat on your plough, in a snow-white
    blouse,
  By the muddy Burn of Shield."

" 'Tis a story that never grows old to me:
  I am crooning it every day,
And I feel I shall tell it in other worlds
  When this one has passed away.

" Long years ago, in my twentieth year,
  A serf on a farm was I:
The ship-throng'd Clyde in the hollow was seen,
  And the city smoked close by.

" The city lay close by the fair green fields—
  Like a toad by a water spring—
And into the vortex of vice I walked,
  And thought it a manly thing:

" I drank of the city's blackest draught,
  Oh! deeper than tongue can tell!
Till I toiled in pain, with a wasting frame,
  And an ever-present hell.

" The celandine shone by the sheltering hedge,
  And the lark sang hid in the sky:
But what were the flowers or the song of birds
  To a wretch so vile as I?

" 'Twas thus one day, long years ago,
  I ploughed in a stubble field,
With a willing team and an easy hold,
  By the muddy Burn of Shield.

" The day was bright, and the great clouds white—
  'Twas April's warmest day;
And the gowans, arrayed in their rosiest tints,
  Were waiting to welcome May:

" When a vision I saw in the broad daylight,
  At the furrow's end afar,
And I stopped my team mid-field to gaze
  Like a bard on a rising star:

" 'Twas a tiny form in a snowdrop blouse,
  With the skirt of the harebell's blue,
And sunny hair of the hazel's brown,
  And cheeks of the gowan's hue.

" And on with a sweetly timid air,
  In the furrow's depth she toiled,
While heavy with clay were her slippered feet,
  And her skirt with the brown earth soiled;

" Till the vision I saw at the furrow's end
  To a gentle child had grown,
With a sweet bright smile, and round her waist
  A coral and golden zone.

" Oh! far from the city's vice I seem'd,
  In a presence so pure and fair,
And I felt 'twas the guiding hand of Heaven
  To save me had brought her there.

" ' And where do you live, little lady,' I said,
  ' And where are you going now?'
' I come but to ask you for leave,' said she,
  ' To walk up and down by your plough.'

" 'But where do you live, little lady?' said I;
        It would have been no surprise
    Had she answered—'My home's where the angels are,
        In the land where nothing dies.'

" 'But yonder is father's house,' she said,
        'Where the silken flag you see,
    And yonder is father's turret tower,
        With white doves on it three.

" 'And yon is our garden wall—within
        The berries are budding now,
    I'll bring you some in the summer time—
        May I walk up and down by your plough?'

" 'Your limbs would be weary,' I said, 'sweet child,
        And sure 'twould be better far
    To *sit* on the plough and be pulled along,
        Like a queen on a royal car.'

" Then sparkled the little one's eyes with joy,
        'Oh! that will be grand,' said she;
    So I made her a seat on the binding bolts,
        And on in the furrow went we.

" Oh! proud was I of my gentle charge,
    And proud of their load were my team;
  But while they were pulling with springy steps,
    I feared it would prove but a dream.

" I feared it would prove but a sweet day-dream,
    As wondrous as it was rare,
  But I never once doubted 'twas Heaven itself,
    To save me had brought her there.

" The April passed and the May day came,
    And oft at my side was she,
  And her presence was ne'er like an earthly thing,
    But a glimpse of Heaven to me.

" A glimpse of the open gate of Heaven—
    I dared my eyes to raise,
  And wished but to live as I might have lived,
    To earn one pure thought's praise.

" No thought had she of the change she wrought,
    Nor aim but a happy hour;
  But her purity was to my new-born wish
    Like the sun and the summer shower.

" It was to my heart like the summer rain
 To the timid and tender flower,
Till the demon that over my thoughts held sway
 Gave place to a holier power.

" The May day passed and the term-time came,
 I came where you find me now,
And only in fancy the brown-haired girl
 Has prattled since then on my plough.

" I see her now as I saw her then,
 Though fifty years are gone,
With her merry smile and her blouse of snow
 And her coral and golden zone.

" I see her now as she sat on my plough,
 And ne'er has she been away,
With her sunny hair and her sinless eyes,
 From my thoughts a single day.

" I see her now with her gowan face—
 'Tis strange that she ne'er appears,
Like a matron lady, sage and grey,
 On the borders of sixty years.

" Wherever I wandered, wherever I toiled,
　　I bowed but to one child-queen,
　And never a face in my heart's love-nook
　　But her's has ever been.

" And even in the Heaven of my dream ('tis strange)
　　Is a burn like the Burn of Shield,
　Where seraphs sit singing on golden ploughs
　　In a silver-stubbled field."

May 10th, 1866.

Last Words.

" OH! Willie, I'm weary wi' waitin
　　Sae lang and sae lanely alane;
　　I'm weary wi' lyin' in darkness,
　　　And thinkin' o' joys that are gane.
I'm painless, an' weel might be patient;
　For a' that I think o' seems clear—
Things in the lift aboon me,
　And things aboot me here.

D

" Ay, Willie, the endless day's dawnin',
    And there are some things I maun say:
Some things that may never be spoken,
    Unless they are spoken this day.
The sum of my moments are reckoned,
    And maybe before the nicht fa'
Ye'll hear the wing-waff o' the angel
    That enters to bear me awa.

" In the sweet buddy May we were married—
    Oh, lichtsome and brief was that year;
But, Willie, e'en then a foretastin'
    O' sorrow at times brang a tear;
For e'en in that year ye were foolish,
    And idle, but hopefu' was I;
Oh, I couldna think ill o' *my* Willie,
    And I said, ' It's a cloud will blaw by.'

" But, ah! 'twas a cloud that lang lingered;
    Oh, Willie, look roun' and see:
I brang ye some gear to be prood o',
    But what in the world noo hae we?

Oh! Willie, gin ilka kind neebor
    Would tak' but the gear that's her ain,
The bed would be bare that I lie on,   .
    And cleedin' oor bairns would hae nane.

" And why are we gearless and naked?
    Oh! think, for it's time ye should think!
Hae ye in sair trouble been lyin'?
    O' an early grave been at the brink?
Or, hae ye been idle and thoughtless?—
    Aye flingin' your wages awa,
And heedless o' what would come owre us,
    Sae lang as a gill ye could ca'?

" The warst was the way o't, my Willie.
    Na, ye maun be patient an' hear—
For that was the wearyfu' way o't,
    Forever frae year to year.
Ay, aye to be sober you promised;
    But aye ye were draggin' us doon,
Aye filling my haun' wi' a penny,
    That shouldna been less than a croon.

" And what was the worth o' your promise?
        At times for a fortnicht ye wrocht,
    Or, maybe, a month at the langest,
        When savin' was a' your thocht.
' Ay, Leezie, we noo maun be hainin',
        E'en hainin' o' meat,' ye would say;
' For, Leezie, oor claes maun be lifted
        As soon as the sillar we hae.'

" Then, Willie, I sinned at your biddin'
        By leevin' a'maist on the win',
    And starvin' my bairns, a' to please ye;
        And what when the wrong had been done?
    What aye was the end o' my sinnin'?
        Wha e'er was the better o't a'?
    When ye, in a fortnicht o' folly,
        Flang a' I had sinned for awa.

" Oh! Willie, my youth's only idol!
        My heaven, and my a' that was dear!
    I fain to the last would speak kindly,
        Sae ye maun be patient and hear.

But memories aboot me are croodin'—
    Ill things that I fain would forget—
I see that it micht hae been better
    For baith gin we never had met.

" Ay, ye wi' a wife should hae buckled
    That aye to hersel' could be true,
That wadna hae borne a' your follies,
    But aye gien her wee things their due,
I should hae been firm as the mountain
    That turns the wild torrent aside.
O, muckle ye needed a woman
    That wisely and strongly could guide.

" Aye flytin'?   I weel micht hae flitten;
    But flytin' I carena tae try;
Wi' kindness I houpit to win ye,
    And kind to you ever was I.
But a' things aboot me grew clearer:
    I see 'twas mysel' 'twas to blame,
For kindness, that tames the fell tiger,
    Aye won me but sorrow and shame.

" Deeper, and deeper, and deeper,
   Aye ye were draggin' us doon!
Ye were shunned by the sober and manly,
   And ever the talk o' the toon.
Pawnin' whate'er ye could carry,
   Beddin' and ocht that was gear;
And pawnin' whate'er ye can borrow,
   E'en while I am lingerin' here.

" Ay, I was to blame for't, I fear me:
   Though leddies baith noble and fair
Hae come to my bed like the sunshine,
   And cheer'd me wi' kindliest care.
Oh, rare are the uncos they bring me—
   For gratitude sweetens them a';
But, Willie, the shame o' my needin'
   Comes in wi' them aye when they ca'.

" Willie, my love and my sorrow,
   Oh, wherefore frae strangers need we?
This is the thing ye maun answer,
   E'en though ye are silent tae me.

Why are we needin' an awmus?
    Oh, say for yoursel' if ye can—
'Wad Leezie frae strangers be needin'
    Gin I had behaved like a man?'

" Willie, my love, ye maun answer.
    Oh, dinna wi' dourness be dumb;
Ye staun' in the licht o' the mornin'—
    To me it's life's gloamin' that's come.
Sae gie me your haun' and your promise,
    Ye'll work for oor bairns and yoursel ;
I fain would hae faith in ye, Willie,
    And joy and bricht days would foretell.

" Weaker, and weaker, and weaker!
    Weaker at night and at morn!
Lang, lang is the road I hae travelled,
    And heavy the burden I've borne!
But nocht were the road and the burden,
    And pleasant the ending o't a',
Gin I could but see how my wee things
    Will fare when their mither's awa.

"Oh! for a glint o' their future
  Fairer than ocht that I see!
Oh! for a glint o' a future
  Fair as for them it should be!
Aye a kind voice, like a father's,
  Calling me hameward I hear;
But aye there's a soun', like the wailin'
  O' wee hungry weans, in my ear."

A Lay of the Twentieth Century.

HER Majesty the Queen sat sad, as many a
      queen has done,
      And thought the world grew darker with
      each rising of the sun,
In spite of all the victories which the men she ruled
  had won.

She saw a fancied ship glide on o'er near and distant seas,

The ship, she thought, that used to brave the battle
    and the breeze,
And dance upon the wildest waves in safety and at
    ease.

But she could see that Doubt stood pale and trem-
    bling at the prow,
And Hesitancy on the bridge, where Promptness
    ruled till now,
And saw the good old ship—a log—through threat-
    'ning waters plow.

Up rose Her Majesty inspired—Minerva in her eye—
" What! shall Rebellion rage unchecked, and my
    good ships close by?
Remove the heads? What then? Why, then, 'tis
    like the trunk would die."

So then she wrote a missive, and she sealed it with
    her seal,
And then she called a waiting lord and low she bade
    him kneel,
" And swear," she said, " you nought of this to mortal
    will reveal."

He strode, he rode, he trained, and sailed, until his
    task was done,
Till the missive from Her Majesty he gave her
    sailor son,
On a calm and moonlit morning, when the latest
    yarn was spun.

"Some rascals have been threat'ning old Parnell, my
    son," it said,
" And Davitt and pale Dillon are, they swear, as good
    as dead;
Well, we would not like to have them die of bullet-
    in-the-head!

" But we could send our *Jupiter* a-steaming anywhere,
And you could go with it, perhaps, and *give them*
    Royal fare!
But never let them roam ashore, for there is danger
    there."

The *Jupiter* is all alive! the fog-horns loudly bray.
The mighty paddles slowly turn; the good ship
    feels her way,

Till her anchor flukes are digging in the mud of
  Dublin Bay.

"Now haste ye, Master Steward!   Take a boat and
  haste ashore,
And board the stores of Guinness—'tis a thing you've
  done before;
Get the best of stout and whisky, and of everything
  galore!"

And then some bold marines went off and guests
  brought more than one,
And when the morning mists fell down before the
  morning sun
They were steaming past the Tuscar, and the Dublin
  raid was run.

Now along the shore of Munster under easy steam
  they creep,
And search the town of Waterford while all the
  police sleep,
And Youghal, where old Ireland saw her first potato
  heap.

And then into the Cove they dropt, and guests from
    Cork were brought;
And some the loyal sailors gagged, and some they
    only caught;
And it seemed, for once in Ireland, they could find
    whoe'er they sought.

Then round to Bantray Bay they steamed; and into
    Castletown
There came a band of sailors when the sun an hour
    was down,—
And they said a brace of irons round a Yankee's
    wrists were thrown.

There was beautiful Kilarney! which they could not
    sail to see,
But they went to bring some butter and a stranger
    from Tralee;
And from Kilrush on Shannon the marines brought
    other three.

So round and round old Ireland, till they came to
    Holyhead,

And from thence the Royal sailor to his Royal
    mother sped:
" And where am I to take them to?" the Royal sailor
    said.

" I've got Parnell and all the O.'s—that ribald
    Yankee too—
  (He has got his legs in irons for the way he spoke
    of you:
But a loyal sailor feeds him. 'Tis as much as we
    can do).

" I've got Dillon. He's been raving; but I think
    we'll bring him round
  (He's a splendid leech, our surgeon, as on water can
    be found).
But I'm not so sure of Biggar; I am afraid he must
    be bound.

" And we've got some reverend Fathers—plucky
    fellows! Full of fight;
They were threatening *Habeas Corpus* and the Pope
    the other night.

But a foretopman has charge of *them*, and they'll be
    snug and right.

" And a score of blackened faces that our sailors came
    athwart,
  We've got safely under hatches, sitting very sore at
    heart,
  For there's not an Irish agent in the ship to take
    their part.

" We've got Sullivan and Sexton, and they only want
    to know
  If we dare to take them anywhere but where they
    want to go;
  And ' It isn't on the sea,' they say, 'a martyr's blood
    should flow.'

" And you say we must remember they are men?
    We'll do our best;
  And each man's to understand he's not a pris'ner
    but a guest?
  And we must not call the worst of them a rascal or
    a pest?

"Good bye!   I need not tell my Lords I'm going, I
  suppose.

I may write you from those waters where your lily-
  namesake grows.*

I'll see my wife, and then we're off, ere anybody
  knows."

Away they steam from Holyhead, and through the
  channel steer.

By Islay and the Hebrides a northward course they
  bear,

Till the smokeless peak of Hecla on the right stands
  bold and clear.

But while they lay off Iceland—there the *Jupiter*
  was slow—

Some guests who had been draining Irish bumpers
  down below,

Resolved to go above and make a patriotic show.

Says bold Parnell, "Who's master here?   And
  wherefore here are we?"

---

* The *Victoria regia*, found in the upper expanses of the Amazon.

"Because," replied his Grace the Prince, "you're
    safest out at sea;
  'Tis the captain that is master, but he takes advice
    from me:

"You came on board to dine. Well! Dine; and
    you'll be set on shore,
  But, while the cook is busy, there's an open sea
    before;
  And a sailor likes to listen where Pacific billows
    roar.

"A sailor likes to listen to the voice of any sea,
  And we have southern wines to get, and fruits from
    Carabee—
  For nothing but the best is found for him that dines
    with me.

"We are going home to Holyhead as straight as crow
    can fly.
  There's many an nasty lump of land before us rising
    high,
  But we're at piece with Neptune, and we'll reach it
    by and by.

"We must not stay at Baffin's Bay nor yet in Davis'
    Strait;
From Labrador we'll round Cape Horn, but there
    we will not wait;
For we must dine at Holyhead, and must not reach
    it late.

"We will anchor off Havana till cigars are brought
    on board,
And a month around Jamaica, I am sure, we can
    afford,
And our steward will discover where the oldest rum
    is stored.

"It is like you fain would linger in the Caribbean Sea,
In and out among the Islands, but I fear it cannot
    be;
For we at Holyhead must dine some time in '83.

"With Neptune at the line we'll drink a bumper to
    the Queen;
And 'tis like the Sea God will insist on shaving
    some one clean;

But we must show you everything that can at sea be
seen.

"But whether we are far at sea, or where we look on
land, .
Remember you're a sailor's guests.   The man who
has command
Is the servant of Her Majesty, and will no nonsense
stand."

"Alas, for poor old Ireland, and the Land League,"
cried Parnell,
"For what may be ere '83 no mortal can foretell."
"And where's my occupation," was the frantic Dillon's
yell.

So, after many a longing look on many a tempting
shore,
The patriot-laden ship was steered to northern seas
once more;
With many a toothsome thing on board, and wines
—a peerless store.

A week they tossed on Biscay Bay and by the shore
of France;

And soon of Cork and Waterford they had a passing
    glance,
As straight they steamed for Holyhead, to anchor,
    dine, and dance.

And then they hailed a Dublin ship, and bade them
    news send round,
That Dillon and Parnell, and all the lost ones, had
    been found,
And were not hid in Spain at all, and neither dead
    nor drowned.

And from the newest "Times" the Prince to all the
    patriots read,
How Irish farmers paid their rents, and all were
    fatly fed,
And how the land was jubilant because the "League"
    was dead.

And then they dined. Ye gods, what wines washed
    down the fish and roast!
"Old Ireland and the Queen," they drank, and every
    loyal toast,

As became a band of "patriots" that knew their
    cause was lost.

And the matin song that from the ship arose at
    dawn of day,
Was a blending of *The Anthem*, " Garry O'wn" and
    " Scots, wha hae;"
And then the guests were landed, safe and sound,
    in Anglesey.

But still the harp of Ireland twangs to many a
    mournful strain,
Of the sailor-raid in '80 and the trip across the main,
And how the leaders of the League were lost and
    found again.

Meditation.

H! mother dear!
    On the last Sabbath of a shadowed year
      Our morning thoughts we turn to thee.
And, as it was in life, we see

Thy face, and think how pleasant it would be
If we might be together, mother dear,
    On this new year.

    Oh! mother dear!
On all the Sabbaths of the coming year
  Our morning thoughts to thee we'll turn;
  And, while we still thy absence mourn,
Within our hearts, the undying hope will burn
That we shall be together, mother dear,
    On some new year.

    Oh! mother dear!
On this bright morning of life's saddest year!
  Dim faces, round thee, we behold,
  Like thine a little, and are told
They are thy children's—in the grave long cold.
  Oh, bring us all together, mother dear,
    On some new year.

My ailing Bairn.

OH! mony a weary waukrife nicht
    Thy troubles, bairn, hae cost me,
  An' aft I feared the morning licht
Would come nae ere we lost thee.
Though Winter sware nae ruth nor care
  Frae's eastlin' blasts would shield thee,
Thou'rt todlin' yet, though weak a-foot,
  Wi' mither's love to bield thee.

The robin in the lonesome wood
  His wooer-sang sings rarely;
The lav'rock through the laigh grey clud
  Salutes at morning early;
An' here and there, on haigh and muir,
  Are weary peesweeps lichtin—
They come to see thy sickly ee,
  My ailin' bairnie, brichten.

The snaw yet haps the nor'lan' hills,
  As winter like as can be;
But yesterday the glens and rills
  Wi' ice were glistering grandly;
Noo, in the dell, the sauch-buds tell
  That Winter's sceptre's broken,
And blythe to me o' health for thee,
  My ailing bairn, hae spoken.

King Frost lay lang amang oor glens,
  'Mang ice and cranreuch dreamin',
But noo he's seen, on distant Bens,
  In snowy robes far gleamin'.
And ere again he comes to reign,
  Wi' blustering, chilling, clangour,
We'll win thee wealth o' ruddy health,
  An' dread his wrath nae langer.

I ken whare first in shelter'd howes
  The celandine will waken;
I ken whare first on sunny knowes
  Uncoils the silken bracken;

An' thee, my bairn, wi' pride I'll learn
   To lisp in sang their praises:
To find thysel' the pale harebell,
   And busk the thorn wi' daisies.

Thy lily cheek, when June shall see,
   She'll spread wi' reddest roses,
And berry-broon thy hauns shall be
   Before the autumn closes.
The constant fear, the frequent tear,
   Thy mirth and bloom shall banish;
For wha could dream this sweet hope-gleam
   May wi' the flower-time vanish.

A Day Dream.

'TWAS summer—July—and the sun had looked
   out
   Just to see what the folks with hay-fields
   were about,
When a man with a paper he saw near a stream
By the sea. " 'Tis some care-tortured mortal a-dream

I will put him to sleep," said the sun, "half a-day.
By my beams!   'Tis the much-abused David
    Macrae."

So he glared at him just as our mesmerists do,
Unwinkingly out of the clear summer blue,
Till down 'mong the grass lay the reader's hot head,
And over his face fell the *Herald* he read.
" More mining disasters," as backward he lay,
Was the heading that last troubled David Macrae.

And whether 'twas that or the sun's fiery heat
(The soft water-lullaby crooned at his feet
Could not cause it), the teller declares he don't
    know;
But the *Herald*-hid sleeper went drop down below,
And in darkness most visible groping his way;
Unto where he knew not stumbled David Macrae.

Then faces—grimed faces, but human—saw he;
Some passed with a smile; some beheld him with
    glee,

And as each form that passed wore some coarse
    woollen stuff—
" Well, it seems that I cannot have dropt far enough:
    For forms just like these in the broad glare of day,
    I have seen where the pits are," said David Macrae.

But onward he moved, and, wherever the track,
Vague danger seemed round him, and all things
   · were black,
Except where some roof-wreathing fungus shone
    white—
A fairy, a ghost, or a halo of light,
Just as fancy elected. " Behold a bright ray
In the darkness Cimmerian," said David Macrae.

But, lo! from a passage a hoarse whispering broke,
" I've a match. Who has pipes?" said a voice, " let
    us smoke."
Then a flame burst before him sulphuric and blue,
And dim haggard forms rushed the passages through
Confusion, death shrieks, and strange torture held
    sway:—
" What! A hell after all?" muttered David Macrae.

And behold! (a new angel within a new sun),
A strange figure appeared as the tumult begun,
Raising high a tall form of concentrated gloom,
It seemed in the roof for its head to make room;
While round it the flame seemed to curl in fond
    play:—
" This is not of earth, earthly," said David Macrae.

And the face was a marvel—majestic, serene—
A face where compassion of old may have been;
And the eyes—wondrous eyes—made for staring
    one blind—
But the glare in them seemed neither cold nor
    unkind,
As a voice, sermon-toned, said, " Where wanderest
    thou, pray?
So, you seek to abolish me, David Macrae?

" I have come just to meet you half-way in the gloom,
And to show how, at times, we earth's hollows illume,
And confuse with faint warmth—you have seen what
    took place,
And how in a moment sweet life we efface;

Just a hint—take it so—of what waits you some
    day."
" Thou wer't ever a liar," said David Macrae.

" A liar! That's brave, and, besides, it is true;
  I'm to others a liar—true Satan to you.
  How I wish we were friends! Just a little me leave!
  Oh! why of his all a poor devil bereave?
  I would live and let live, as among you they say."
" No! I can't compromise it," said David Macrae.

" Ah, me! Do but think, sir, how hard it must be,
  The sweet souls of infants no more come to me.
  Once they poured down in thousands from east and
      from west—
  From wherever the foot of Transgression found rest;
  Now the dear little spirits are sent t'other way"—
" 'There was never one near you," said David Macrae.

" Ah, well! very good, reverend brother, but sure
  You might well let the torments of adults endure
  Through eternity—so 'twas arranged long ago;
  And a bargain is always a bargain, you know—

Oh! leave that fond fear to grace sermon, and lay"—
"No; I've done with such error!" said David Macrae.

"Well, brother—for I am a minister too,
  And, just like yourself, do what's set me to do;
  I have fought in my time; so have you;—very well,
  Here's a list of your Synod.   For each I've a cell,
  Kept aflame from the first for him—what do you
      say?"
" I confess I am mortal," sighed David Macrae.

Then laughter burst forth from the long-lingering
    flame,
Now distant it echoed, now nearer it came—
A sneering, triumphant " Ho, ho!   Oh, ho, ho!
How they love, these Seceders!   Amen!   Be it so!
What is sauce for the gander is sauce for"——
        "Away!
'Twas a moment of weakness!" cried David Macrae.

Then while still in his ears the strange ho! hoing
    rang,
From his couch by the streamlet the pale dreamer
    sprang

In a visible tremor, and wild was his stare,

And tragic the grasp of his hand in his hair,

"What a horrible vision!   Thank God, he's away!

'Twas a dreadful temptation!" said David Macrae.

Tam Troker.

WHEN TAM TROKER was wee,

If he got a bawbee,

He aye had some place that he
kent o' to hide it;

And, as soon's he had ane,

Some bit plan would begin,

To get just anither to slip in beside it.

He was aye in the street,

Wi' bare head and bare feet,

And nane e'er could say that his garments were garish

He would rin in his sark

To secure an hour's wark,

And a horse-hauder like him was ne'er in the parish.

When he gaed to the schule,
He was ne'er sic a fule
As to fancy a "reddie" a profitless plaything;
Aye his cry was "plunk fair,"
But he plunkit wi' care,
And he ne'er geid a bool to a neebour for naething.

And there ne'er was a preen
Could escape Tammie's een,
As it lay on the pavement on market or fair day;
For a preen, every day
He had heard the folk say,
Would sell for a groat o' guid sillar at Ne'arday.

And when bairns o' his size
Showed some grand "glessie" prize—
Though sair he was tempit and bother'd aboot it—
He micht hae a wet e'e,
But he kept his bawbee—
He likit the "glessie," but managed withoot it.

When the candie-man cam,
He made aye fun o' Tam,
And swore sic a customer never was yokit;

But he ne'er gaed awa
Till a farthing or twa,
For banes or for rags, wi' Tam Troker he trokit.

But ye maunna suppose
Tam was e'er ane o' those
That will "*tak*" if the happer says "Tak it, man, tak it;"
He lo'ed sillar, 'tis true,
But, to gie him his due,
He could want it until he could honestly mak it.

How he hained, how he thrave,
How he pushed by the lave,
How fast in his teen-time his pennies were bankit,
Is a thing o' the past,
But his memory will last,
And for his example he ocht to be thankit.

And though it is true
That the lot 'tis o' few
To rise and to soar as Tam Troker ascended--
Aye wi' een lookin' up,
Drainin' Fortune's full cup,
In hainin' the maist o' our ways micht be mended.

"Though I canna leeve free
O' my neebors," said he—
"Crusoes with their fine-fruited isles are but scanty—
Yet, wi' naebody's plack,
I'll put claes on my back;
And wi' naebodys flour I'll put scones in my pantry."

"If guid wine makes me fain,
I'll hae wine o' my ain;
If guid meal makes me yaul, I will buy't frae the miller;
And, to buy my wean's shoon,
When the auld anes are done,
I am safest to gang wi' a neevefu' o' siller."

Are they here that ken Tam?—
Weel, they ken he's nae sham,
But a steive sturdy carl wi' a place in creation;
And 'tis men sic as he,
Wha can hain when they're wee,
That keep healthy the credit and nerve o' a nation.

F

A Natal Lay.

" **L**ET me sing a Birth-day Ode !"
　　　Thus does each adorer cry
　　　When this natal day draws nigh.
Should Apollo deign to nod,
　　Straight is raised the frenzied eye—
Spins the humming top of rhyme
All about this natal time.
But when I my boon besought
Grave Apollo nodded not,
And, alas ! I well could see,
All the Muses stared at me,
And the whispered wonder came,
" What is this aspirant's name ? "
Down my head in sorrow hung,
And the Ode remains unsung.
Sitting then with soul subdued
To a vexed and fretful mood,
" Why," I said, " an Ode at all,
　　That may flat as snow-flakes fall ?

Why the yearly rite maintain
Of a eulogistic strain—
Setting *one* within the maze
Of an oft-repeated praise,
Round and round to toil astray
On a feastful natal day?—
While his peers impatient sit
Longing till electric wit
Forth shall leap with flash divine
' 'Mong the walnuts and the wine.'
Till the 'Ode' again achieved
Leaves their tortured ears relieved?
Nay, although it fell not flatly,
As a snow-flake falls, but patly
Touched the temper of the time,
And in warm and lofty rhyme
Told again the well-known story—
What increase were there of glory
To the Bard whose songs to-night
Shall the gravest cares make light?"
So, imagined be the strain
That should tell you o'er again
How the *man* we meet to honour

Wooed the maiden Fame, and won her;
How he loved, and how men loved him;
How the test of trouble proved him;
How the fervour of his pen
Thrilled, and thrills the souls of men;
How he woke by rill and river
Echoes that will ring for ever;
How, whate'er he stopped to name
Shares the marvel of his fame;
How, of him it may be said,
" Nothing that he touched is dead; "
How, although detractors cry
" Much that he has touched should die; "
Yet, where'er his foot has been,
Plodding pilgrims aye are seen,
Who believe there yet remains
A gleaning of ungathered grains—
Verses bold and warblings sweet—
Which shall make his fame complete.
Thus, in an imagined strain,
Each may tell the tale again,
In the pause of speech and song,—
Or fancy-led may roam among

Hallowed scenes by Ballochmyle,
Logan Water, Doon, in Kyle,
The Banks of Ayr, or Afton Braes.
And where'er the fancy strays,
Singing bird or blossomed sod
Be the subject of an Ode—
Each one musing as he may,
On the Bard we praise to-day.

Lochranza.

AN EJACULATIVE POEM.

(To be read with a Scotch accent.)

H ay! we'll to Lochranza hie,
  Be fair or foul the weather,
  And hear the whaups and shepherds
   cry
Through mists amang the heather;
And see doon "foaming from the fells,"
 That for our eyes have waited,
The stream that still of freedom tells
 With ardour unabated.

We'll rise and see the morning sun
   Amang the vents grow broader;
But we the early boat will shun,
   That wakes the river odour.
And we will train it safe and swift,
   Our " Heralds" deftly skimming
The while our thoughts before us drift,
   Our path with pleasure trimming.

We'll see the Cart that once was clean,
   The bridge (to be) we'll fancy;
And docks, and wharfs, and ships we'll ween
   The work of *Necromancy.*
Lochwinnoch and its swans we'll see,
   Lochbirnie and its rushes;
And Garnock winding through the lea,
   And gleaming through the bushes.

The moonworts on the hills of sand
   We'll pass, but we'll not see them;
To some wild *cryptogamic* band,
   With *vasculums,* we'll lea' them.

Oh ! shame to take a blade of green
   From knolls so bare and barren !
But there's the shore and dim sea-sheen,
   And there's the way to Arran.

And now we from the harbour steam,
   And now we're in the channel—
An eastern wind comes swift behind,
   And pierces coat and flannel.
But where is Arran? where the peaks
   That fill the soul with wonder?
The eye in vain an answer seeks—
   We may as well go under.

For wheresoe'er on weary feet
   The gold of time we're squandering,
There still must come a time to eat,
   Or brief will be our wand'ring.
So down we go to feast below—
   In fear and wonder eating—
Till " Brodick Bay," we hear one say,
   " Let's up and do our greeting."

Yes, this indeed is Brodick Strand—
    We've landed and we've paid for't;
Some other scribe with less in hand
    May say what's to be said for't.
For we are to Lochranza bound—
    In famous trim for trudging—
And far away, ere fails the day,
    We'll supper find and lodging.

"And is the Isle so empty then?
    One kindly glance would please us."
"Why! there is Reid, the best of men—
    This way he looks! he sees us!"
"Now sunshine on our path shall be,
    See, half across 'tis gleaming;
An eye that's kind's the sun for me—
    It sweetens work and dreaming."

"What? walk? the way is steep and far,
    And ye are of the city;
With over-toil the day to mar
    Would surely be a pity.

There's Corrie Car !" "That thing so frail?
    So obsolete, 'yet tender.'"
"Our Queen to it entrusts her *mail*,
    And that's our very gender."

"But see! already in the box
    A gent. and lady seated."
"Too late! too late! ah! cruel fate!
    But let us bravely meet it."
"Sir, have you room for us?" we say;
    He grins, his brown teeth showing,
"'Tis not what room I have," quoth he,
    "But what's the number going?"

Away! away! around the bay
    With stately pace we're driven;
Ourselves are three, four more we be,
    And therefore "we are seven."
And there's the eighth, our Jehu bold,
    Across the splash-board straddling;
The ninth that beast, though first yet least,
    Between the traces waddling.

"Oh! day divine!" "Oh! reckless nine!"
    'Mid many a joke were saying,
As now the splash-board skyward tilts,
    And now we're seaward swaying.
But Jehu, tugging at his steed,
    Has not a thought of jesting;
His load to-day for luck may pray,
    For he his springs is testing.

And so the case he calmly views,
    And tugs and shouts and whistles;
He knows he carries Scotland's news,
    And Arran's love epistles.
And surely *we* are nothing *new*—
    The pheasant walks before us;
The heron stolid stands in view,
    The blackbird whistles o'er us.

The lordly deer and lady doe
    But raise their heads to greet us,
And lambs, like animated snow,
    Come dancing down to meets us.

The rabbit 'mong the myrtles feeds,
    And of·him hears us speaking;
To-day·no brute a stranger heeds,
    Nor flies, a shelter seeking.

But, ah! there comes a time, ye deer,
    Ye gentle does be ready—
There loometh one with shotted gun
    Towards you pointed steady.
Ye pheasants learn from man to flee—
    Yet, why this lapse to sadness?
Even dukes must die; let you and I
    Devote this day to gladness.

So all again is grand and fair,
    Still thus we would be driven;
Still thus would cling, and chaff, and swing
    From Brodick on to Heaven.
But while we vow to put our drive
    In trim and rhythmic story,
We stop, get down, and gladly own
    We're safe at last at Corrie.

PART SECOND.

We lingered on the Corrie Strand,
　For lingering well rewarded;
We heard the wild sea thrill the land
　As never mortal heard it.
The monarch boulder on the beach
　Could not be passed unheeded;
Some lesson it is there to teach—
　We never tried to read it.

Around it lambs, in friendly strife,
　Were racing as we passed it;
And mighty death and fragile life
　Were ne'er so well contrasted.
But not to moralise come we,
　Nor muse on Styx and Charon—
To be from smoke and thinking free
　Is why we came to Arran.

We saw the Sannox downward reel,
　And foam and flash and glisten;
Well-pleased emotions new to feel,
　And not to talk but listen.

How pure the golden margined rills—
 The glens were nought without them;
And whence that silken film the hills
 To-day have thrown about them?

Be silent! there the peaks repose!
 Can this be adoration?
And, as we climb, behold how grows
 The wond'rous transformation.
Yet something does the fancy seek—
 The grand to mystic turning—
Some *form* to stalk from peak to peak,
 In brazen armour burning.

Their names? these mighty masses named,
 Like tower-lets in a burgh?
It should not be—but we shall see
 A map, perhaps, to-morrow.
Meanwhile a thirst pervades the air—
 That's not to be disputed—
We'll taste the stream that wimples there;
 And let it be diluted.

And here our weary limbs we'll rest,
   Like Jove, our clouds compelling;
This water is the very best,
   Loch Katrine's own excelling.
What matter if the changing sky
   Suggests a change of weather;
For, hark! at last the shepherd's cry!
   The whaups' and his together.

Is that it all? a drink; a smoke;
   A stroll where streams are gleaming;
A little easing of the yoke
   Of thought; a maze of dreaming.
A glimpse of foggy peaks; a sense
   Of uncommitted leisure—
Is that the rare concomitance
   That makes the day a pleasure?

But that, and nothing more, we own,
   Yet never fools were gladder;
See there the fairy burn comes down,
   And there, by Jove! an adder!

Quick! strike! Poor brute! how limp it lies;
  What pity that you hit it;
Ah, yes! but when the devil dies,
  The devil will be pitied.

And has our path by death been cross'd?—
  Too fervid was our gladness;
And, lest we should go home and boast,
  There comes this touch of sadness.
'Tis ever so—where'er we go
  The waves of Fate come after,
With grief upon the crest of one,—
  On that that follows laughter.

No matter! we the burns have seen,
  The shepherd's dogs have patted;
We've praised the mountains grey and green—
  Have with the shepherd chatted.
And every stream appears to gleam
  The brighter for our sipping;
And on with glee towards the sea—
  The way we go—is tripping.

Who prophesied 'twould rain to-day ?
   How poorly he's been gifted—
For " o'er the hills and far away "
   The cloud he feared has drifted.
And there's our haven for the night !
   Thy kindly care, Lochranza,
Till morn we'll claim, and syne, thy name
   We'll weave into a stanza.

PART THIRD.

Awake ! upon the dusty road
   The clouds their stores are pouring ;
The lark sits murmuring on the sod,
   Afraid of skyward soaring.
The storm that's rushing down the strath
   May wheel to Tobermory,
But, in the face of it, our path
   Is o'er the hills to Corrie.

No ! not for us the morning dram
   That spoils the mood supernal ;
We'll break our fast.   What, eggs and ham !
   Are eggs and ham eternal ?

Not even one little, little fish,
    Nor fresh, nor salt, nor reestit;
Nor even the native "aiten dish,"
    On which the gods have feastit.

Our bill! let's see how much we've got
    To keep in trim the body;
What's this? There's some one had a lot
    Of halfs! and here's some toddy!
Have we been at our country's curse?
    " Perhaps, but *I* am stronger;"
" And *I* am not a whit the worse,"
    " And *I* am ages younger."

Farewell! good host! we'll come again;
    We've had some splendid raining—
So good, that some of us would fain
    Arrange about remaining.
We seek not, Sovereign Nature, here
    Your wild free will to fetter;
But might the blast behind us veer,
    It surely would be better.

G

We climb the steep with steady pace—
　　Still darker clouds are lowering;
And still the blast that hits the face
　　Is streams about us showering.
How grand were now a thunder-burst,
　　With lightning flashing o'er us;
Or, if a water-spout were thurst
　　From out the clouds before us.

No palate-parching dust to-day
　　From every footfall rises;
No sparkling streamlet by the way
　　To rest and taste entices.
A royal rain! a thorough drench!
　　Let's troll a line together;
Ten thousand rills foam down the hills,
　　And burst frae 'mang the heather.

Enough, ye kind condensing fogs,
　　Of patterings and of plashing;
The sheep, the shepherd, and the dogs,
　　Have had a bounteous washing.

The breasting of a storm so rare
   Our limbs is strongly taxing;
But see! the torrent in the air
   Is surely thinner waxing.

And has it ceased to rain at last?
   Unsling the wallet leathern—
Our thirst has been increasing fast,
   Let's pledge the birks like brethren.
And there's a finely-filtered rill
   Among the myrtles oozing;
What's that you say?   A better day
   You would not think of choosing.

Come on! come on! 'twill rain anon;
   Ach! there, as vile as ever,
The brute that shocked us yesterday;
   Away! it makes me shiver.
The watershed! two tiny burns,
   Twin sisters, there are parted;
Each lingers looking back, and turns
   And murmurs broken-hearted.

Behold again the unwearied sea
 Beneath the rain cloud streaming ;
Essays once more to swamp the shore—
 " And that's the heron screaming."
'Twas thus he cried above the flood
 That drowned a world for sinning :
" Hark ! scream the third ! Prophetic bird,
 The second flood's beginning."

" Oh ! sea ! thou ever varying dream !
 Creation's grandest mourner ! "
Enough ! I know a nobler theme—
 Our inn is round the corner.
There's Corrie's parlour, and its fire
 With visioned comfort coming ;
Then in(n)ward, Ho! we'll dripping go,
 Of coming comforts humming.

PART FOURTH.

Indeed we've to Lochranza been,
 We've trudgéd hence and hither,
And have a double sample seen
 Of royal highland weather.

We've been and seen—what have we not?
  But, lass, it has been raining;
So let us have some whisky hot
  The time our duds are draining.

And we shall dine if soon we may—
  To fast we shall be sorry;
Yet we have but an hour to stay,
  And then we fly from Corrie.
Meanwhile, the whisky hot, sweet lass—
  Be sure the water's boiling;
And let us, gently warming, pass
  To rest from hours of toiling.

Oh! happy hour! to hear it pour
  Without—no drop abating;
Why should we fret if some get wet
  While we are snugly waiting?
But there's the dinner bell—we'll dine,
  With appetite abundant;
This roast is prime, this stew's sublime,
  And everything's redundant.

Our chariot is at the door,
   The charioteer is waiting;
And now we're under rain once more,
   Of future aches debating.
No doe to-day delights the eye,
   No antlered forest rover;
"The brutes, like every thing that's wise,
   Of course, are under cover."

"Oh, yes! it is a gallant steed,
   And, though he might be fatter,
No storm fears he, nor flood, nor sea—
   Oh, yes! he's used to water."
"He once was swam for life and won."
   "Oh, yes! and did not rue it;
So, should it rain as thick again,
   He's sure to pull us through it."

"And here's his Grace! He looks like one
   That had a noble ettle,
And grand historic work had done."
   "But then he's only metal."

" There's Brodick Pier ! at once embark,
　　Cease, prancing brute ! wo, woa !
We'll have to call our ship the ' Ark '—
　　Yes ! and the captain, ' Noah.' "

But where's the captain and the ship ?
　　Away ? we can't believe it ;
He could not pass the harbour slip
　　And none of us perceive it.
" Och ! never fear ! she'll soon be here,
　　No use at all complaining ;
She longer stays on rainy days,"
　　" But this is more than raining."

See how the waiting shed is packed !
　　What gloomy, fretful faces ;
Those folks are sure that they endure
　　Some frolic of his Grace's.
Omnipotent ?　Of course he is !
　　No Arran boat dare linger
A moment on a day like this
　　Would he but lift his finger.

But there's our boat! Our *wait* is past!
　With glee the crowd's infected!
Like everything that comes at last,
　She comes when least expected.
And so our trip is o'er.　Adieu!
　Ye peaks unseen and barren;
On deck remain—'twill cease to rain
　As soon's we're clear of Arran.

Enough! it is enough!　We moan
　And murmur unregarded;
The weather clerk neglects our groan,
　Or else he has not heard it.
Our pilot, stolid as a stone,
　Keeps through the torrent peering;
Good soul! he shall not sink alone
　If he astray is steering.

But why upon a theme so sad
　Still harping?　Does it matter?
So wet, you say, " Well, so you may—
　You have been under water."

" Yes, I have drank it with my air—
    My pants are soaked and shrinking ;
'Tis water, water everywhere."
   " But most of it's for drinking."

Oh for some rare nepenthean draught !
    To keep the life-stream flowing—
Light up the face, and sadness chase,
    And set the limbs agoing.
Oh for some wizard-woven lay—
    Some charm, howe'er unholy—
To pierce, with smile-creating ray,
    This cloud of melancholy.

Ardrossan ! What? in port at last
    With not a soul amissing?
We'll find our train, defy the rain,
    And leave the boat our blessing.
How pleasant has the journey been—
    How free from tiresome tameness ;
But pleasanter by far, I ween,
    Without that streaming sameness.

Awake, thou daring sleeper! wake!
　　Thy bones to ache thou'rt dooming.
"What's that?" "The grinding of the brake."
　　"And yon?" "The *Suburb* looming."
Ah! home, sweet home!　How gladly we
　　Shall stretch and rest to-morrow;
And dream of dreaming by the sea,
　　In nooks that know not sorrow.

Song.

Air—" *The Pretty Maid Milking her Cow.*"

THE lav'rock that sings in the Trongate,
　　A kin' body loot him awa;·
But back cam' the bird to the Trongate,
　　A' fluttering, an' liken to fa'.

"Noo, whare hae ye been, my braw birdie?
　　Sae spak' his auld mistress, sae kin';
"And 'tw'y are ye back, my braw birdie,
　　To fret by a winnock o' mine?"

"Oh ! I was awa at the Cathkins,
        A-flirting wi' Flora hersel';
    A-wading 'mang flowers on the meadows,
        And drinking frae mony a clear well.

" But nocht could I hear on the Cathkins
        But birds, and the souch o' a tree—
    And sae I cam' back to the Trongate,
        Where naebody warbles like me."

"Oh blythe I'm to see ye, my birdie—
        I had ye before ye could flee ;
    But he frae the Cathkins that brocht ye
        Is sleeping beneath the saut sea.

" And fain, for his sake, would I keep ye,
        But freedom is dear to us a'—
    Sae aff to the Cathkins, my birdie,
        And mate wi' the best o' them a'."

    The birdie sprang licht to her shouther,
        And happily gleamed his brown ee—
" And what lacks a birdie o' freedom,
        Wha sings to a mistress like thee ?

" I'll nae mair awa to the Cathkins,
 Though pinkies blaw thick on ilk lea.
But sing 'mang the din o' the Trongate,
 Where naebody warbles like me."

The Dorty Bairn.

P RESERVE me! Lizzie Allan,
  Ha'e ye no your breakfast taen?
Sic a face ye hae wi' greetin'!
  What's the matter wi' ye, wean?

Ay! a flee ran owre your parritch?
 Fanny snowkit at your bread?
My certie! Leddie Lizzie,
 Ye're a dainty dame indeed!

But, the parritch can be keepit,
 And the bread can be laid by :
An', if hunger proves nae kitchen,
 Then the tawse we'll hae to try.

Ay! a bairn may weel be saucy
  When there's plenty and to spare;
But there's mony a better lassie
  Wad be blythe to see sic fare.

Oh! waes me! but it's vexin',
  Yet it's needless tae misca';
See, there's the glass! What think ye?
  D'ye ken yoursel' ava?

There's the een I praised this mornin'
  For the happy licht within,
Noo as red's the fire wi' rubbin'—
  Baith as bleart's the cloudit moon.

There's the pina' that an hour sin'
  Was as white's the driven snaw,
Noo as draigelt as the dish-clout—
  D'ye ken yoursel' ava?

An' your hands that were like lilies—
  Saw ye e'er sic hauns as thae?
An' your cheeks! their verra roses
  Ye'll hae rubbit aff some day!

Oh Lizzie, Lizzie Allan !
  ' Ye maun mend, or ye shall learn
That it's mair o' cuffs than cuddlin'
    That awaits a dorty bairn.

Ye've a kiss tae gi'e me, hae ye ?
    Ye've a kiss as weel as him ?
Oh thae e'en ! there's nae resistin',
    When it's sorrow makes them dim.

Ay, ye'll get anither pina',
    An' I'll kame your curls sae broon ;
An' ye'll be my ain wee Lizzie,
    An' the best in a' the toon.

Mea.

MEA ! blithesome Mea !
    Goes slowly down the glen—
A-listening to the blackbird
    And the genty wren

Every note and twitter
 Fills her heart with glee ;
Mea ! rosy Mea !
 Who so blithe as she ?

Mea ! rosy Mea !
 Lilts from bower to bower—
A wealth of pleasure finding
 In each passing hour.
Still trustful of the present—
 Nor fearing what may be ;
Mea ! guileless Mea !
 Who so blithe as she ?

Mea ! lithesome Mea !
 Of rambling feats can tell
By lonely moor and mountain,
 Dark tarn and rocky fell.
And she can boast of angling,
 But still, averse to pain—
The trout her skill secures her
 She aye throws back again.

Mea ! fearless Mea !
  On the cliffs can stand,
Where she, leaning forward,
  Sees the sea-washed sand.
Kaes peer out beneath her,
  And flowers, beyond her reach :
As she longs to flutter
  Down towards the beach.

Mea ! wondering Mea !
  Sitting in the bay,
A-listening to the rollers,
  Dreams brief hours away.
And well she knows the roaring
  Of the great wave nigh,
Ere her feet it reaches,
  Will dwindle to a sigh.

Mea ! ardent Mea !
  In all that's tasteful speeds
See, she deftly changes
  Into flowers those weeds.

Ask her, and she'll lead you
　To the sun-touched pool,
Where the weeds were tossing
　When the tide was full.

Mea! sloe-eyed Mea!
　Far away from home,
But a little longer
　'Mong these hills will roam;
Flowers and leaves will wither,
　Birds and sea will mourn,
When she to the city
　Must again return.

Mea! tireless Mea!
　Roams from morn to e'en,
Where a stranger rarely
　On her path is seen.
Sea-gems in her satchel,
　Sea-flowers in her hand—
What so fair as Mea
　On the pebbly strand?

H

Nay ! she's not my Mea !
   I my best have seen;
And she has left behind her
   But her first sweet 'teen.
But, when love has found her,
   Still my song would be—
Mea ! rosy Mea !
   Who so blithe as she ?

Cochno Braes. *

AMANG the braes whare Cochno rins,
   Owre boulders brown, and ferny linns,
   'Twas aye my wish my rest to win,
When a' the sword could do was done ;
And aye I hoped I micht be laid
Beneath the peacefu' beechen shade,
Whare safe the cushie broods and croons,
Amang the braes whare Cochno rins.

* Suggested by the story of the imprisonment of one of the
Hamiltons of Cochno, in or about 1568.

The bonnie braes whare Cochno springs,
Whare owre the loch the lavrock sings,
Through mouldy roof, and boleless wa',
Amid the mirk I see them a'.
Aboon the clank o' weary chains,
Aboon the taunting trumpet strains,
I hear the soaring bird that sings,
Aboon the loch whare Cochno springs.

The breeze that blaws frae Cochno braes,
Within my dreary dungeon strays,
And fain would Cochno's master tell,
O' hawthorns white in ilka dell.
But, ah! the halesome breezes there
Shall lift my haffet locks nae mair,
My hunting horn again shall raise,
Nae echo blithe on Cochno braes.

Oh aft my waefu' fancy sees
A reek that curls aboon the trees,
And ase-flakes like the hawthorn's snaw
Fa' thick round Cochno's burning Ha'.

A wife an' weans frae fire that flee,
And need the help my han' should gie,
Cauld courin' 'neath the moaning trees,
And driving smeek my fancy sees.

And 'mid the wail frae Cochno braes
I hear my struggling country's waes;
A ruthless faction reigns supreme,
And far and near the war-fires gleam.
As round a peerless pris'ner Queen
The fate-mist lifting slow is seen;
Aye wilder wails and darker days
I hear and see on Cochno braes.

Oh turn thou breeze that seaward strays!
And speed thee back to Cochno braes!
Tak' health to a' that loe me there,
And joy to her that's a' my care.
Oh tell nae how I pine and fret!
But say there's hope o' freedom yet;
Fu' welcome ocht will be that says
I'll soon return to Cochno braes.

Song.

Air—"Cadder Fair."

OH! guess ye what the deil did
    When bonny May lay sleepin'?
He cam', an' wi' his gruesome lips,
    Aboot her mou' kept cheepin'.
He tried to touch her dimpled chin,
    An' owre her leer'd sae fainly;
She tried to rin an' make a din,
    But tried, puir lassie, vainly.

"Oh! sweet's your mou'," the deil said
    (The loon her mou' had pree'd na),
"An' fair's your face," the deil said
    (An' weel I wat he lee'd na).
"Doon mony a mile's my dreary ha',
    An' joy we feast on scantly;
A maid sae rare would cheer us a'—
    In faith, we canna want ye!"

"Put on your claes," the deil said,
　　"I canna aye be waitin';
　The lass that scorns a faithfu' lad
　　Maun e'en put up wi' Satan."
　She, greetin', rase and got her claes,
　　Her heart—his grin was breakin't;
"Come, come," quoth he, "let's downward flee,"
　　And then she screeched and wakent.

'Twas ae guid turn the deil did:
　　As soon as Sandy kent it—
"Dear May," said he, "ye mine maun be,
　　Or ye'll some nicht repent it."
　And 'deed, against a plea sae fair
　　She never thocht o' threepin;
　And gruesome clootie comes nae mair
　　To kiss her when she's sleepin'.

The Pointsman Grim.

OME, stir up the fire! for the light is too dim
To sit in, and hear of the pointsman grim,
Whose deeds filled the papers of country
and town,
And every one knows that his name was John Brown

He had a sweet wife, had this grimmest of men,
And a child—but he wasn't a pointsman then,
But bent for his living each day o'er his awl—
And the dream of his life was a well-stocked stall.

One day, to his wife, giving bank-notes three,
" Dear Jane, you must go to the country," said he,
" You're thin, and you're pale, with this life in the town,
So go to your mother's, get plump, and get brown."

Out spoke Mrs. Brown, and she spoke with much sense:
" Consider, my husband," said she, "the expense."
Said John, " You must go," so she spoke not again,
But she packed up her things, and they went to the train.

John went to the train, and he saw them away,
" Good-bye, my own Jane "—that was all he could say;
He did not kiss her, but he kissed their dear child,
And whispered, "You'll give it to mother," and smiled.

So the train moved away, and he went to his stall,
And whistled light-hearted all day o'er his awl;
But at night, when he purchased his *Citizen*, there
He saw, in huge letters, "A Dreadful Affair,"
And read, "A Collision," good God! with the train
That had left in the morning and carried his Jane.

So he rushed to the station, the whole truth to know:
The story was just as the *Citizen* said—
A blunder to ruin the train had betrayed!
And the shoemaker staggered and said, "Just so!"

John went to the scene, and he bowed down his head,
And he spoke no reproaches, but buried his dead;
But he never more smiled—what was life now to him.
"And why should I live?" said the pointsman grim.

The dead and the *debris* had been cleared away,
And the Press and the Pulpit had both said their say;
And the railway directors had met to agree
What damages paid to the public should be;
They didn't quite say so, but this was their thought—
"It stands not to reason that we should pay aught."

And so, when they read—" Wife and child of John
    Brown,"
" Oh, a shoemaker fellow, quite poor, in the town !
We'll give him, let's see," said the chairman, and smiled
" A fifty for her, and a ten for the child."

John got their grand offer, and read it, and stood,
With a flash in his eye and a fire in his blood—
" My wife valued fifty ! my child valued ten !
Just so ! its all right !" said that grimmest of men.

So off to the railway directors he went,
And took off his bonnet and low his head bent—
" I'm out of a job, my good masters," said he,
So make me a pointsman, and you shall go free."

"A pointsman!" said they, "very well, 'tis but fair,"
And John had a compliment paid from the chair;
So they wrote the conditions—John wrote "I agree,"
And duly installed as a pointsman was he.

Then they gave him a box—gave him flags red and
    white—
The red one for danger, the white for all right;
And they showed him a handle to shove to and fro;
"Be careful," said they—said the pointsman, "Just so."

"But what would occur," said the pointsman, "if I
Should the handle hold *thus* when the train's passing
    by?"
"If the train's going down when you hold it," said
    they,
"It safe with its human freight goes on its way."
"And where would it go if I held it *there?*"
"Into the wrong line—and God knows where!"

So then with his duties they left him alone,
And the trains for a fortnight had come and had gone
And now in the darkness, and now in the light,
He let them pass safe with their human freight.

Yet, often he muttered, "O that I but knew
When that generous chairman was passing through ;
For this is the gate of Destruction," said he,
"And I am the devil that keeps the key."

Till one day, to him, kindly, a surfaceman said,
"Have you heard there's a lot of new lyes to be made?
Well, the chairman and others, they say, will come
  down
To-morrow by special express from town.

"Have everything tidy, for sharp is the eye
Of the railway chief as the special goes by ;"
And the pointsman he answered, "Of course, just so,
And the chairman shall go—where he ought to go."

So home went the pointsman and went to his bed,
And he saw his own wife in a dream, and she said—
"O John, if this dreadful thing you do,
The dream you've been dreaming may never prove
  true.

The dream you've been dreaming will prove but a
  dream ;
You ruinward float like a fly on a stream—

Like a rudderless bark o'er the ocean driven—
For murder was never a passport to heaven."

But the pointsman grim was'nt frightened a bit—
He saw the sweet spirit away from him flit;
And, waking, he muttered, "She's gone, just so,
But the chairman shall go—where he ought to go."

Then out came the pointsman at break of day,
And when anyone spoke he had nothing to say;
But he oiled his points and his lamps put out,
And picked up the coal which was lying about.
And nobody fancied, and nobody knew,
What the desperate pointsman was going to do.

Till far away, in an hour or less,
He heard the scream of the first express;
So he threw down his red flag and pulled out his
     white—
Turned off the red signal and showed them "all right."
And then, when he saw her come thundering along,
He rushed to the points, and he held them wrong.

Then into the siding she rushed amain,
Where waiting at peace stood a shunted train—
A crash, and a shriek, and a fearful cry,
While the engine seemed climbing her way to the sky.
Then the voice of the pointsman was heard—" Bravo !
The chairman has gone where he ought to go !"
And then, when the force of the engine was spent,
Away from his point-box he quietly went,
Where a great crowd had gathered, of old and young,
And he was the burden of every tongue.

But nothing cared he—he but stooped his head,
And peered in the face of the dying and dead ;
But the face of the chairman he could not find,
For nothing was there of director kind.

Then round on his heel turned the pointsman grim,
For the dead and the dying were nothing to him ;
To his own house he went—by-and-by to his bed,
When in came the county policeman and said—
" You seem to be taking it cool, Mr. Brown—
Get into your clothes, sir, you're wanted in town."
Said John—" I suppose they will give me my due—
But it wasn't the thing I intended to do."

So John was examined, imprisoned, and tried—
They found he was guilty, and something beside—
They found that a mad-house the place was for him—
And there was an end of the pointsman grim.

MORAL.

Let people who sit in high places be sure
That life is no dearer to rich than to poor
The truth of this proverb will never be dim
To all who remember the pointsman grim

Wee Wattie.

EED, we a' but thocht shame,
   When wee Wattie cam' hame,
   That sic a bit neivefu' should mak
   sic a steer ;
  E'en his granny hersel'
  Hadna seen nor heard tell
O' onything like him for mony a lang year.

  And sae sure were they a'
  He was wearin' awa
As gently as dew frae the flowers on the braes,

That they grudged to be fashin'
The wee thing wi' washin',
And thocht it was cruel to load him wi claes.

No ! it wasna the gladness
O' gain, but the sadness
O' losing, we saw in ilk kin' neebor's ee ;
An' the house lay in gloom—
In shadow o' doom—
Nane ventured to hope but his mither an' me.

We praised him, and blessed him,
An' soothed an' caressed him,
An' sang to him aft wi' fou heart an' moist ee ;
An' jeered at the croakin'—
Sae cauld an' provokin'—
O' a' that were fearin' wee Wattie wad dee.

Oor hearts aft were sair
Wi' a bye-or'nar care ;
An' aft cam a demon, malignant an' grim,
An' tauld a fell tale
O' hoo Death would prevail,
An' filled, for the moment, grief's cup to the brim.

But ance when the curst
Demon whispered his worst,
An' sneered aboot christ'nin' as useless an' vain,
A smile, like the licht
O' the first star o' nicht,
Brack ower the sweet face o' oor soun'-sleepin' wean.

It needed na that
To inspire us, I wat,
Wi' new love for the wee thing, but faith it inspired;
An' aye as we tended,
We hoped that he mended,
An' rase frae the dreechest o' watches untired.

*   *   *   *   *   *

Yon's the laddie ye see—
No sae won'erfu' wee—
An' yon are his schule books, a dozen or mair;
An' he'll sune be a man,
That sae feebly began
His lang journey uphill, an' mak pleasant oor care.